My Faithful Friend

DESIGNED BY RONI AKMON

COMPILED BY NANCY AKMON

WRITTEN BY KAREN CHOPPA

ILLUSTRATIONS BY GRE`GEREARDI

BLUSHING ROSE PUBLISHING

SAN ANSELMO, CALIFORNIA

FOR:

_____

FROM:

_____

DATE:

_____

COVER ILLUSTRATION AND INTERIOR ILLUSTRATIONS BY GRE` GERARDI. THESE ILLUSTRATIONS ARE REPRINTED
WITH THE PERMISSION OF THE BALLIOL CORPORATION. TEXT WRITTEN BY KAREN CHOPPA.
DESIGNED BY RONI AKMON
COMPILED BY NANCY AKMON

ISBN# 1-884807-61 5

BLUSHING ROSE PUBLISHING
P.O. BOX 2238
SAN ANSELMO, CA. 94979
WWW.BLUSHINGROSE.COM

PRINTED IN CHINA

YOU ALWAYS MAKE ROOM FOR ME IN YOUR LIFE

You always help me out

You're sweeter than candy!

You're so likable

When I'm sad, so are you...

...BUT YOU'RE QUICK TO CHEER ME UP

EVEN IN STORMY TIMES YOU MAKE ME FEEL SAFE

You try so hard to be good. Me, too!

YOU'RE LIKE FAMILY TO ME

You try to get along with everyone

You always share

You like surprises, too

You can keep a secret

You're never jealous

You're at home in my Sunday-best times...

...AND IN MY BLUE JEAN DAYS

DRESSING UP AND MAKE BELIEVE ARE MUCH MORE FUN WITH YOU

WE TAKE CARE OF EACH OTHER

YOU HELP ME MAKE NEW FRIENDS

You're quick to forget my mistakes

You can be very gentle

SOMETIMES TROUBLE JUST FINDS US...

YOU MAKE EVEN RAINY DAYS FUN

You're a willing dining companion

You're very trustworthy

Sometimes you're quiet...

...AND SOMETIMES YOU'RE "BOUNCY"

WE HAVE THE SAME MISCHIEVOUS STREAK

THERE'S JUST NO STOPPING YOU

YOU PUT THE "HAPPY" IN HOLIDAYS

WITH YOU, EVERY DAY'S A PARADE

You're just so huggable

AT THE END OF THE DAY, YOU'RE STILL BY MY SIDE

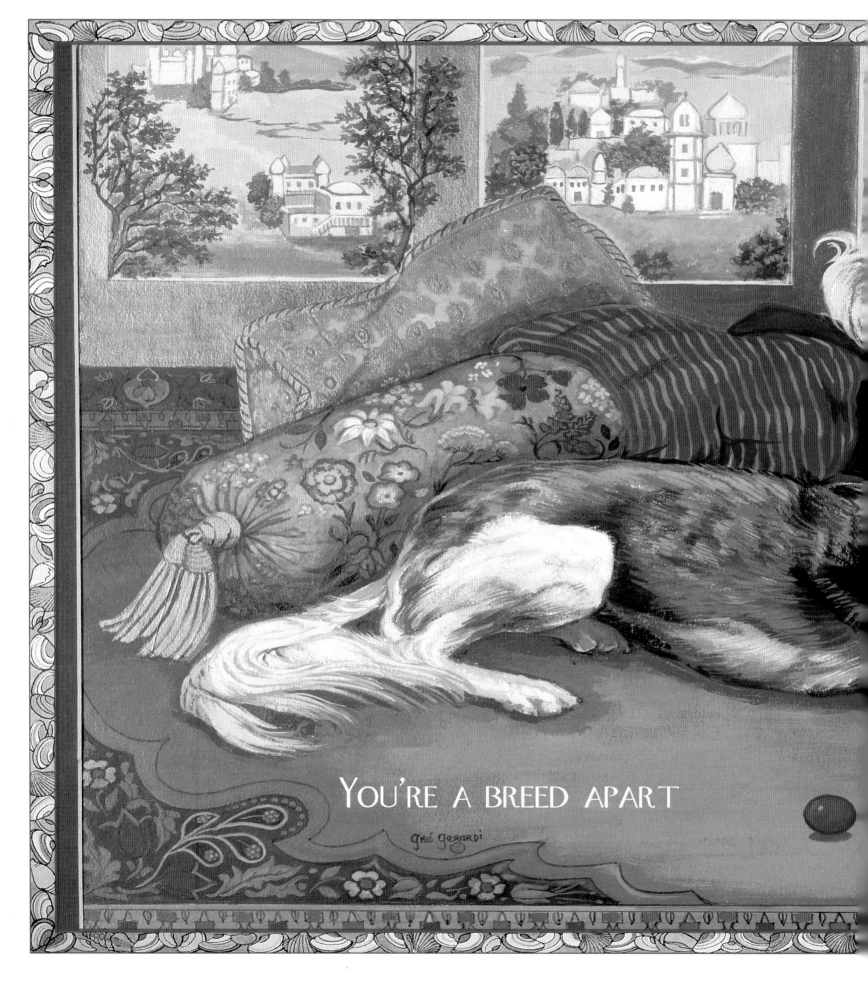

You're a breed apart

gré gerardi

YOU'RE MY FAITHFUL FRIEND